T0128442

A Letter to Ellen

A Story of
The Declaration of Independence Desk

As told by
Grandfather Thomas Jefferson

by

MARYANNA TAYLOR VAUPEL

A Letter to Ellen

A Story of The Declaration of Independence Desk As told by Grandfather Thomas Jefferson

iUniverse books may be ordered through booksellers or by contacting:

iUniverse
1663 Liberty Drive
Bloomington, IN 47403
www.iuniverse.com
844-349-9409

ISBN: 978-1-6632-2407-1 (sc)
ISBN: 978-1-6632-2409-5 (hc)
ISBN: 978-1-6632-2408-8 (e)

Library of Congress Control Number: 2021914152

Print information available on the last page.

iUniverse rev. date: 07/12/2021

PREFACE

In 1963, the author was a graduate student at Salisbury College. An assignment for a Methods of Social Studies course offered an interesting challenge. How can robust historical research be represented creatively? The author discovered that Thomas Jefferson had a craftsman in Philadelphia build a portable writing desk for him to use while he was a member of the Continental Congress in the years leading to the founding of our nation. Research on the artifact led to this creative project, an imagining of Jefferson fondly reflecting on his time using the desk to advance the cause of the American Revolution.

Research revealed that Thomas Jefferson indeed wrote a letter to his granddaughter, Ellen Wayles Randolph Coolidge (1796-1876), and her husband, Joseph Coolidge (1798-1879), to describe the writing desk, a consolation wedding gift to replace a separate gift that was lost at sea. With the help of the internet and the availability of primary sources and documents, original letters were found.

The story had quietly waited all these years for the author to finally have it published. Even though it was customary in those times for personal correspondence to be addressed to the male, the author is taking the liberty to keep this letter addressed to Ellen, as it was when this creative endeavor initially took shape.

Th. Jefferson gives this Writing desk to Joseph Coolidge
Jr. as a Memorial of affection. It was made from a
drawing of his own by Ben Randall, cabinet maker of
Philadelphia, with whom he first lodged on his arrival
in that city in May 1776. And is the identical one on
which he wrote the Declaration of Independence.
Politics, as well as Religion, has its superstitions,
these gaining strength with time, may one day, give
imaginary value to this relic for its association
with the birth of the Great Charter of our Independence.

Monticello. Nov. 18. 1825

FROM THOMAS TO JOSEPH COOLIDGE, 18 NOVEMBER 1825

Monticello. Nov. 18. 1825.

Th. Jefferson gives this Writing desk to Joseph Coolidge jun as a Memorial of affection. it was made from a drawing of his own, by Ben Randall, cabinet maker of Philadelphia, with whom he first lodged on his arrival in that city in May 1776. and is the identical one on which he wrote the Declaration of Independence, Politics, as well as Religion, has it's superstitions. these, gaining strength with time, may, one day, give imaginary value to this relic, for it's association with the birth of the Great charter of our Independence.[1] [sic]

Monticello, November 17, 1825

To Ellen, my beloved granddaughter,

I do hope that this finds my newly-wedded granddaughter in good health. I send my best wishes and hearty congratulations to Joseph and welcome him into our family.

For your wedding present, I had one of our craftsmen build for you a lovely writing desk. However, news has reached me that the vessel on which I had shipped the desk was lost in a storm at sea. In place of that desk, it is my decision to send you my writing box. I have carried it with me for many years and many miles, but I do not use it much anymore since poor health limits my writing.

Since you, my dear, always seemed so interested in your granddad's affairs, I think perhaps you might enjoy the story that this little desk knows so well.

Let me reminisce. The year was 1776, and the place was Philadelphia. At that time, I was thirty-three years old, a tall, red-haired, blue-eyed gentleman from Virginia. I was there as a delegate to the Continental Congress.

I had a comfortable room, except for the heat, at the Graff Boarding House. However, a desk which was comfortable and convenient for me was not available. Therefore, I asked Benjamin Randall, a cabinetmaker there in Philadelphia, to build this portable desk for me. It was very handy to carry around and a safe place to keep my papers and writing tools as the drawer locks.

On this desk, I wrote a document for Congress. It is now called the Declaration of Independence. What did this document mean? Why did we declare ourselves free? The reasons are many, and I can only briefly tell you in a letter.

England was using the colonies as a source of raw materials and as customers for the manufactured products. The colonists did not appreciate this as the profits were going to the mother country. To add to this, England placed taxes on many articles coming into the New World. The colonists refused to pay these taxes, and British soldiers were sent over to enforce these acts. The result was the Revolutionary War. In June of 1776, the *Minutemen,* as the untrained volunteers were called, and the British soldiers had battles at Lexington and Concord.

The delegates from the colonies were gathered in Philadelphia. They were joining together in an attempt to solve these problems. On June 7, Richard Henry Lee made a great resolution in Congress. It stated that, "The United Colonies are, and of Right ought to be Free and Independent States."[2] He was saying that the colonies should separate from the mother country. Earlier, Patrick Henry of Virginia also made a very daring statement when he said, "Give me liberty or give me death."[3]

You can quickly see how the people felt and what they really wanted to do. The delegates soon realized that they were not succeeding in solving the problems with the mother country in a peaceful way. So they decided that it was time to take action if they wanted to become free and independent.

Three days after Lee's suggested resolution, Congress appointed a committee to write a paper to tell the mother country and the rest of the world the reasons for declaring our independence. The men on the committee were Benjamin Franklin, Roger Sherman, John Adams, Robert Livingston, and myself. The members selected me to write the paper. No, I did not use any books or notes. They weren't necessary. It was not my job to invent new ideas. I just wrote what the people had on their minds and tried to give it the tone and spirit of the time.[4]

When I finished, Benjamin and John read it over. They made a few changes but on the whole were quite pleased.

The paper was presented to Congress on June 28. Other committee reports and items of business had to be taken care of first. Midsummer heat and flies, however, hastened our proceedings.

On July 2, the Congress again took up Lee's resolution. It was discussed and finally voted upon. Twelve colonies were in favor of it. New York, the thirteenth represented, would not vote. Later, however, they were in favor. This decision was actually the cutting ties with the mother country. The written declaration was the way of telling England.

The order of business for the third of July was the declaration. Before discussing it, however, we had to consider the requests from General Washington and other officers for supplies. They were in great need of men, food, and ammunition. Finally, we debated the paper. It had to be read and discussed, changes considered or made, and read again. Congress did decide to strike out several statements. The first was the criticizing of the people of England. We still had friends in England which we wanted to keep. The second was the anti-slavery clause. The delegates made changes in the interest of colonial harmony. The northern and southern colonies had held different opinions concerning this point, so they left it out completely. The delegates realized that this was the time they must work together.

The debating had to be carried over to the next day. When the debate was over, we took a vote. It was unanimous. It pleased me very much, when upon hearing the final reading, Benjamin Franklin said, "I wish I **had** written this myself."[5]

In spite of the hot, muggy weather, the pestering flies, and choking tobacco smoke, everyone felt relieved when the vote was taken. The unfamiliar sound of the words, "A Declaration by the Republic of the United States of America in Congress Assembled," rang in our ears. Now that we had officially cut the ties, we must be united.

John Hancock, the president of the Congress, was the first to sign the declaration. While writing his name in big, bold letters, he said, "His Majesty can read my name without his glasses." [6] It may surprise you, my dear, but the other delegates did not sign their names on July 4. Almost a month later, on August 2, the rest of the members of Congress signed. Even then they were kept secret until December of that year.

As Benjamin Franklin signed, he was heard to say, "Indeed, we must all hang together. Otherwise, we shall most assuredly hang separately."[7] He, as well as the rest of Congress, realized that if we did not win the war, our signatures on that declaration would be proof of high treason, the punishment of which would be hanging.

On Monday, July 8, the declaration was read to the public. Many people, young and old, gathered within hearing distance of the State House.[i] The people were pleased with what they heard and gave cheers or praise which developed into celebrations in all the colonies. I have long remembered the ringing of the tower bell. It proclaimed to the land the birth of a new nation. The bell truly seemed to be ringing out its own inscription, "Proclaim liberty throughout the land to all the inhabitants thereof," which is found in the twenty-fifth chapter of Leviticus.

By the way, if you are in Philadelphia, Ellen, stop by and see that old treasure. If my memory serves me correctly, it is twelve feet around the base, and weighs more than 2,000 pounds. To the British, it would have been a source of ammunition, but in 1777, it was secretly taken to Allentown. There it was hidden under the floor of a church, Zion Church, I believe. A year later it was returned to the State House. The grand old bell has been rung every year since on the Fourth of July and on very important state occasions.[ii]

That first celebration was a long, continuous one as the news reached each of the colonies. Because of slow transportation and communication then, it was a month later when Georgia finally received the news. Three months later, it arrived in England.[iii]

And now Ellen I shall give you a brief summary of that paper that I wrote on this little writing box.

The first paragraph gives the purpose of the document. It states that the people have a right to set up their own government. Since we firmly believe that all men are created equal, it was necessary to break away from the mother country. The people of the colonies had submitted to conditions which they didn't feel were fair.

The next part of the declaration is a list of grievances to the king. There are twenty-seven of the charges, ranging from the Stamp Act to the Quartering Act.

The last paragraph declared us free and independent of the mother country. It was a restatement of Lee's resolution. And finally, the signatures of the delegates.

Well, my dear, I have written much and have grown weary. The old writing box has stirred my thinking of the past which I'm writing to you. "The old desk itself claims no merit of particular beauty. But its imaginary value will increase with years. And if you newlyweds live to be my age, you may see it carried in the procession of our nation's birthday."[8]

Good health to you and Joseph. I wish you a prosperous and fruitful marriage.

Much affection,

Your grandfather,

Th: Jefferson

TO THOMAS JEFFERSON FROM JOSEPH COOLIDGE, 27 FEBRUARY 1826

Boston: Feb 27. 1826

Dear Sir,

I have deferred too long to mention the valued memorial which you sent me: several times, however, have I written to thank you for "the Desk," and as often destroyed my letter least that, which was but the sincere expression of gratified feeling, should seem to you like exaggeration: but I was truly sensible of the kindness of the gift, and the compliment it conveyed:—the desk arrived safely, furnished with a precious document which adds very greatly to its value; for the same hand which, half a century ago, traced upon it the words which have gone abroad upon the earth, now attests its authenticity, and consigned it to myself. When I think of this desk, "in connection with the great charter of our independence," I feel a sentiment almost of awe, and approach it with respect; but when I remember that it has served you fifty years—, been the faithful depository of your cherished thoughts; that upon it have been written your letters to illustrious and excellent men—your plans for the advancement of civil and religious liberty, and of Art and Science; that it has, in fact, been the companion, of your studies, and the instrument of diffusing their results;—that it has been the witness of a philosophy which calumny could not subdue, and of an enthusiasm which eighty winters have not chilled,—I would fain consider it as no longer inanimate, and mute, but as something to be interrogated and caressed.[9]

Joseph Coolidge Jr

EPILOGUE

The Declaration of Independence desk did arrive safely to Jefferson's beloved Ellen and family. They fully realized that it was a *precious relic* and cherished it for many years. Their descendants donated it to the nation in 1880. It can now be viewed in a position of honor at the Smithsonian National Museum of American History — complete with its dents, scratches, and ink spills.

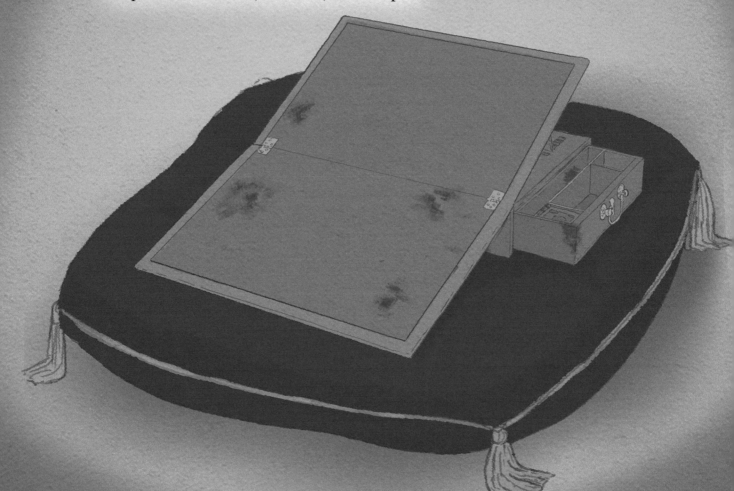

FOOTNOTES

1. Thomas Jefferson. *From Thomas Jefferson to Joseph Coolidge.* National Archives https://founders.archives.gov/documents/Jefferson/98-01-02-5674.

2. George E. Ross. *Know Your Government.* (New York: Rand McNally and Co, 1959) 8.

3. Ibid 7

4. Henry Steele Commager and Richard B. Morris. *The Spirit of Seventy-Six.*, Vol I, (New York: The Bobbs-Merrill Company, Inc. 1958), 315

5. Cornel Lengyel. *Four Days in July: The Story Behind the Declaration of Independence.* (Garden City, New York: Doubleday and Company, Inc. 1958), 165.

6. Ibid. 250.

7. Ibid. 253.

8. Ibid. 296.

9. Joseph Coolidge. *To Thomas Jefferson from Joseph Coolidge.* 27 February 1826, Founders Online, National Archives. https://founders.archives.gov/documents/Jefferson/98-01-02-5939.

END NOTES

i. It was not called Independence Hall until after 1828. Jefferson died in 1826, so he referred to it as the State House.

ii. The last ringing of the bell was July 8, 1835, when it cracked while being tolled for the death of Chief Justice John Marshall.

iii. The telegraph was not used until the 1840s.

BIBLIOGRAPHY

Bedini, Silvio A. *Declaration of Independence Desk: Relic of Revolution.* Washington, D.C.: Smithsonian Institution Press, 1981.

Coolidge, Joseph. *"To Thomas Jefferson from Joseph Coolidge, 27 February 1826," Founders Online,* National Archives, https://founders.archives.gov/documents/Jefferson/98-01-02-5939

Commager, Henry S. and Richard B. Morris. *The Spirit of Seventy-Six.* Vol. I. New York: Bobbs-Merrill Co, 1958.

Jefferson, Thomas. *"From Thomas Jefferson to Joseph Coolidge, 18 November 1825," Founders Online,* National Archives, *Declaration of Independence.* Garden City, NY: Doubleday and Company, Inc., 1958.

Ross, George E. *Know Your Government.* New York: Rand McNally and Company, 1959.

Small, Lawrence M. *Mr. Jefferson's Writing Box.* Feb 2001 cd., Smithsonian Magazine, 2001.

EPILOGUE # 2

How pleasant it is, at the end of the day,

No follies to have to repent;

But reflect on the past, and be able to say

That my time has been properly spent.

Jane Taylor

Source: *The Way to be Happy*, page 527, **The Oxford Dictionary of Quotations**, Oxford University Press, 1953.

Fifty-eight years later, the story is published and the author received a beautifully handcrafted replica of the writing desk.

(Thank you, Ben!)

Printed in the United States
by Baker & Taylor Publisher Services